DAD BOD REBEL

A BBW & SINGLE DAD ROMANCE

LANA LOVE

LOVE HEART BOOKS

For more books by Lana Love, please visit:

https://www.loveheartbooks.com

To read the rest of the **Dad Bod 2.0: Large and In Charge** series, please visit:

https://www.amazon.com/dp/B0BVRQHN7C

CHAPTER 1

MARSHA

can't believe a man hasn't snapped you up yet, Marsha," my best work friend, Helen, says as she unboxes her lunch and unfolds her napkin.

I roll my eyes, but I smile anyway. "Maybe I'm too much of a handful for them."

Helen chuckles. "Or maybe they don't appreciate a strong, independent woman who has standards and knows what she wants."

"That's nice of you to say, but I'm okay with not dating right now."

Helen gives me the side eye as she picks up her sandwich. "You say that, but I don't believe it's true. We've got a veritable stream of handsome single men coming through the school with their children. Why not date one of them?"

"Oh, no," I say, holding up my hands and leaning back in my seat. "I don't think so. You know my rule – no dating single fathers. I don't want a man with the baggage of an ex-wife or a widow. And I'm not sure I want to date a man with a child. I've seen friends try to navigate that, and it never seems to go well. I don't think I have the stamina for it."

"You've got a fair point about the excess baggage," Helen says with a nod. "I still think you should give some of these men a chance. I bet there's a diamond in the rough out there. You can always find enough good qualities in a person to make up for bad habits or things that aren't ideal. Just this morning, I saw a father dropping off his daughter. No wedding ring, but he looked like he could be a model, especially dressed in the sharp suit he was wearing."

I laugh and shake my head. "I don't think a man like that is going to be interested in me. I'm not sure I'd be interested in a man like that."

"Then who would you be interested in, Marsha?" Helen narrows her eyes.

I know I've given away that I've actually considered this, even though I say I won't. "I'm not sure, but certainly not someone who thinks everything has to be perfect. I'd love a man who works with his hands. There's something pure and honest about work like that."

Helen arches an eyebrow. "Well, there are plenty of blue-collar men here in Jefferson. I bet my Victor knows someone he could introduce you to."

"No!" I exclaim. "No offense, but blind dates don't work for me. Men see I have," I gesture down at my large breasts and wide hips, "and they immediately tune out. Either that or they think I'm easy and can just use me and toss me aside."

"Pssh. They're fools if you ask me. Real men like a little meat on their ladies." Helen shakes her head at this like she doesn't believe me. I love that she thinks it would be so easy for me to find a man to love and let into my life, but I don't think she understands the reality of dating these days.

"If I can find a single dad like that, I'd consider it," I concede. I'm not sure I believe I would actually do this, but I can't deny that I would rethink my rule if a man came along and just swept me off my feet.

Even though I only started teaching at Jefferson High this year, Helen and I have had this exact conversation more times than I can count. I've learned that giving slight concessions or appearing to is the best way to stop her from setting me up on a blind date.

"Would you date these fathers if you were single, Helen?"

Helen has been happily married for twenty years. Sometimes I think she doesn't realize what it's like to be single anymore, especially these days. I'm not even thirty yet, but it seems like all the men on apps are looking for someone younger – and thinner – to start a relationship with. Even older men, who I generally prefer, want the same type of women. It's challenging and disheartening, to say the least. I don't like being single, but right now, it's the best option for my sanity.

"Of course I would," she says, though I see uncertainty in her eyes.

"Yeah, well, maybe I'll think about it."

Helen looks at me, and we both know I'm fudging the truth, at least a little bit. The thing is, I don't know if I could handle a man's baggage if he had an ex-wife, especially if it was a vindictive divorce. Or if he was a widow. I mean, how do you step into the shoes of a dead woman? Especially if it was someone he really loved? I'm not sure I'd want another woman's ghost to be the third person in a relationship or marriage.

Right now, the children I teach are standing in for the children I don't have, and that's perfect. I get to help shape these kids' lives, and hopefully, they'll help the world be a better place. For now, that's enough.

Or at least this is the story I tell myself.

* * *

"TESSA, can you stay after class, please?"

A chorus of *oohs* echoes in the classroom as the other students tease Tessa for being asked to stay late. I smile at Tessa as she walks toward me to let her know she's not in trouble. Not that she ever would be, because she's probably the most talented student I've ever had.

"What's up, Miss Andrews?" Tessa asks, her eyes wide as they meet mine.

"Have you given any more thought to applying to the summer writing program I mentioned? I think you'd be an excellent fit for the program. Your last story was amazing."

"Thanks, Miss Andrews," Tessa says.

She looks down at the ground, but I can see her smile, and I know she's proud of what she's done. She's shy, but writing is where she shines, and it's where she lets her personality and her soul come through.

"I don't know about the program. I mean, it sounds good, but I don't know."

When I look at Tessa, it's clear there's something she's not saying. I've seen this in a lot of students because they don't have confidence in themselves. Sometimes it's because of other reasons.

"Why not, Tessa? We've talked about this before. Your writing is exceptional. A program like this will push you further, and the people you meet can help open doors for you in the future."

"I don't know, Miss Andrews. The thing is, I'm not sure my dad would agree."

"What do you mean? He must be so proud of you. Haven't you shown him your grades and my comments on your work?"

"I have," she sighs. "But he's not supportive of me wanting to be a writer."

"That's nonsense," I say before I can check myself. I try not to comment on parents and their parenting styles. But parents who say creative writing or the arts aren't worthwhile tick me off. Life isn't worth living unless we have art.

"Why don't you let me talk to him?" I tell Tessa. "Sometimes, if they hear from a teacher, it can make more of a positive impact."

"I don't know. He can be a hardass." She covers her mouth, latently aware she's just sworn in front of a teacher.

"It's okay. I'm not going to punish you for language. Just don't make a habit of it, alright?" I smile kindly at her.

Helen says I give my students too much leeway with language, but an occasional outburst in private isn't a big deal as long as a student isn't swearing in every class.

"Okay, did you tell him about the writing program?"

"I did. He said absolutely not. No effing way would he let me go to a program like that in the summer."

I sigh in frustration, and my fingers grip my pen so hard that my joints ache. "Did you tell him I recommended this for you?"

"I did," Tessa says, her voice wavering again. "He said it doesn't matter. He said that writing is a hobby, not a career. And that it's foolish for me to get my hopes up by going to some fancy writing program."

"Tessa," I say, working hard to keep my voice level and professional, "can I speak with your father?"

"Miss Andrews, I don't think you want to do that." I hear the concern and weariness in her voice, but it only makes me want to stand up for her even more. I can't stand by and watch a parent kill the creative life force in another student. It never ends well for anybody, especially the student.

"Are you sure about talking to him?" Tessa repeats as if trying to give me a way out of talking to her dad.

"Yes, Tessa. I'm sure. Can you call him?"

"Okay," she says slowly and pulls out her phone. "Hey, Dad. No, everything's fine. I'm with one of my teachers. She wants to talk to you," she says, her voice muffled.

A masculine voice grumbles something in the background, and Tessa hands me her phone.

"You the teacher?" he barks without saying hello. Great. Just what I need – another father who clearly thinks he knows my job better than I do.

"I'm Tessa's writing teacher, yes. Are you Tessa's father?" This isn't the first time I've been on the other end of a phone with a father who sounds gruff and intimidating, and I know it won't be the last.

"Yes."

"Okay. Will you be attending the parent-teacher conference tonight?" I ask, doing my best to control my voice.

"I wasn't planning—"

"Change your plans. We need to talk."

CHAPTER 2

ROMAN

*Y*ou got a girlfriend you're not telling us about, Roman?" Mack teases as I return to the old Chevy I'm working on and get back to work on its engine.

I don't even bother looking at Mack because winding me up is his favorite pastime. "You're making me a broken record, man. You know I'm not dating until Tessa goes to college."

"Yeah, yeah. You and your ass backward rules. You used to love the ladies." Mack laughs and shakes his head.

"I did. I still do. But my deal with Tessa is neither of us will date until she's out of high school. Besides, she doesn't need a stream of women coming in and out of her life like that. Not after what happened with her mom leaving her like she did." I grip my wrench so tightly my knuckles pale and work the wrench to loosen a nut on this old engine. "If you must know," I glare at him, "it was one of Tessa's teachers."

"Uh-oh. Everything okay with your girl?"

"Tessa's fine. You wouldn't believe the crazy idea she's gotten into her head. Thinks she wants to be a writer. She's got this teacher convincing her to pursue a career in writing and wants her to go to some dumbass summer writing program. And now she's just had her teacher call me." I curse under my breath.

I look at Mack, nearly banging my head on the hood of the car as I stand up. Rage bubbles up when I see him chuckling under his breath. "What the fuck, man? I thought you'd be on my side. You think this is funny?"

"Tessa's what? Thirteen? Fourteen years old?"

"She's fourteen." I nod.

It still surprises me that I suddenly have my daughter in my life. I didn't even know she existed until I left the Army and my ex dumped Tessa on me. *It's your turn now,* is what she said, unceremoniously leaving Tessa on my doorstep. I've never regretted welcoming Tessa into my life but adjusting to being a dad has had many challenges. It's been years, but now she's a teenager, it feels even more like I have no idea what I'm doing.

"First, you better watch it with that wrench. You're going to break something you don't want to pay for if you're not careful there. Second, man, maybe you should give her a chance. See if she has any talent."

"Mack, dude. Come on. You think she's gonna make it as a writer? I love Tessa, but damn, she gets these ideas in her head."

"Yeah, you need to give her a chance. Let her try it, and if she flames out, be there to catch her."

"What the fuck, Mack? I thought you'd be on my side. You go and get soft, man?"

"Roman, no, I'm not soft. You know that. What I have are three sisters. You can only say no for so long before they rebel in a dangerous way. Believe me; you don't want to lose Tessa from your life. My parents tried so hard to make my younger sister someone she didn't want to be that she nearly ran away and never came back. That's a nightmare I wouldn't wish for my worst enemy. In the end, it worked out, but it was a long time before Cecily fully trusted our parents again."

I look at Mack and consider what he's said. I sure as hell don't want to lose Tessa or worse. "Well, I guess we'll find out. I talked to the teacher last night. Tessa told her I said she couldn't go to this fancy pants summer writing program. And then the teacher wanted to talk to me. Can you believe that? Like she thinks she's going to change my mind!"

"You should talk to her and actually listen, Roman. She's a teacher. It's her job. If she says Tessa has talent, she's probably not wrong."

"Kids today are too soft. They weren't in the military like we were. They expect things with not a lot of work. I don't want to see Tessa get hurt. I want her to have a good life and not to lose herself in some romantic idea of being a writer and then have it all come crashing down because it doesn't work, Mo."

"Yeah, man, I get it. Like I said, give her a chance to try it out. It won't end well If you keep saying no to everything she wants to do."

I grumble. "Well, I guess I'll find out. I'm meeting her at a parent-teach conference tonight. She had the nerve to tell me I *had* to attend. What the fuck, man?"

Mack laughs again, which does nothing to reduce my frustration. "Good luck with that, man."

* * *

"Stop looking like I kicked a dog, Tessa."

I already know tonight is going to end with my Tessa performing a humongous sulk. There is nothing that prepares you for a child's entry to adolescence, especially when said child only recently came into your life. Tessa is a sweet girl and usually behaves well, but...she's rebelling against me, and I honestly don't know how to manage this. I double down on telling her the best path, but we get further into a hole.

On the other hand, she's definitely my daughter. Her stubbornness tells me she's my blood, aside from us having the same hazel eyes and red hair. It didn't take a DNA test for me to know she was my child.

"There she is! Miss Andrews!" Tessa's mood changes instantly as we walk into the large school lunchroom.

She jumps up and waves her arm, trying to catch the attention of this teacher she's been raving about. Only thing? I don't see who her teacher could possibly be. What I do see in the general direction Tessa is looking is an absolute bombshell of a woman. The woman has thick, wavy brown hair and is wearing a dress that is almost obscene in how it hugs the curves of her body. Everything is covered, but fuck, I want to run my hands over her skin and feel her move with my body.

Dammit, Roman. You gotta follow your own rules. No dating until Tessa is in college.

11

"Where is this teacher of yours?"

"This way, Dad." Tessa grabs my hand and pulls me across the crowded lunchroom. More than a few women look at me in that assessing way single women do. It's like I have a sign that says Single Dad hanging around my neck.

The only thing more frustrating than my daughter right now is when single moms swarm me at school events like this.

"Tessa! I'm so glad you could make it!"

I turn my attention to the voice talking to Tessa, surprise filling me as the bombshell I was just fantasizing about pulls my daughter into a bear hug. When they pull apart, I blink twice. How is a woman who looks so young old enough to be my daughter's teacher? Then I remember our conversation earlier, and my blood pressure rises again.

"Dad, this is Miss Andrews."

"Roman," I say, shaking her offered hand firmly.

"It's wonderful to meet you. Tessa is incredibly talented."

I pause for a long moment. "Thank you. I'm glad she enjoys writing. It's a good hobby."

Miss Andrew and Tessa share a look, and I recognize the sulky expression in Tessa's eyes. *So help me if she causes a scene.*

"Mr. Alston," she says, ignoring that I gave her my first name. "Have you read any of your daughter's stories?"

I shift my weight, uncomfortable. I haven't read a book since I was in school, and I've never seen a reason to change that. Books are fine...for other people. "I read one," I admit. "It wasn't bad."

"See? I told you – he doesn't even care!" Tessa's voice rises an octave.

I mentally start counting to ten. "Tessa! This is not the time or the place," I warn her, looking at all the people around us and wondering if anyone is eavesdropping. Being undermined by my own daughter in public is not something I tolerate, and she sure as hell will hear about it later.

"Mr. Alston. You're doing your daughter a disservice by not reading her stories and encouraging her to pursue writing. I'm not lying about your daughter's talent."

I admire that Miss Andrews meets my gaze and doesn't look away. Despite the scene my daughter is starting, this woman is either ignoring it, or she's one of those patently annoying women who are always happy.

"What do you know about good writing? Hm?" I challenge her, crossing my arms over my chest.

To her credit, she matches my stare and doesn't blink or flinch. "My experience is wide-ranging. In addition to being a published fiction writer, I also spent several years as a technical writer."

"A technical what?" I can't keep the bite out of my voice. As much as I love Tessa, this feels like being sandbagged.

"Technical writer. You know, like manuals and instructions. That kind of thing. Someone has to document how things work," Miss Andrews explains patiently.

Is she fucking with me? She meets my gaze and doesn't back down, which I grudgingly admire. Most women look at me and shrink away. I know I can be intense, and I respect that she's standing her ground.

I think back to the Army and all the goddamn manuals we had to read and memorize. "Yeah, we had a lot of those when I was deployed."

"Exactly. Who do you think prepared them? People like me, though I didn't work on military contracts. It's a wide field, though. Some people think about technical writers as writing software documentation, but it can also be for manufacturing, corporate research, or marketing materials. Or it can be work in the government or military sectors."

"Huh." I pause for a moment and consider this. The possibilities start opening in my mind. If Tessa could be convinced to also study something alongside creative writing, she could have a solid career plan.

"Yes," she says, "'huh' is right. I understand where you're coming from, but I think you should learn more about the possibilities. Tessa is an excellent writer, and it should be encouraged, not deprioritized."

I glare at Miss Andrews. Who the hell does she think she is? I'm used to people falling in line and following orders, but neither Tessa nor her teacher got the memo.

"Look," she continues. "There's a writing open house on Thursday night. There will be a variety of professional writers there to talk to students about the different paths they can take. It's usually open to college seniors, but Tessa should go, and so should you. I guarantee you'll be surprised at the career paths available to Tessa."

"Dad, please?" Tessa pleads, bumping her shoulder against my arm and looking at me with hopeful, puppy dog eyes.

"I'll think about it."

CHAPTER 3

MARSHA

*H*ow did it go last night for you?" Renee asks, pulling a sandwich out of her lunch bag.

I raise my eyebrow at the sandwich.

She smiles so wide I think her face is going to split. "It's gluten-free, silly! Coop has been working on new bread recipes. I was missing sandwiches, so he's been experimenting with recipes that are compliant with my diet that actually taste good. This one is my favorite so far. Have I mentioned how much I love the man?" Renee beams at me, love written all over her face.

My heart yearns for the kind of love she shares with her husband. She and Coop met when she interviewed him for the Raytown Reporter for a newspaper feature. She has an autoimmune disease and has a long list of foods she can't eat, so he opened a new bakery location and made it completely gluten-free and compliant with everything she can and can't eat so she could eat baked goods without getting sick. He goes out of his way to ensure the needs of Renee, and other people who can't eat gluten, aren't overlooked.

"Your husband is the best." I smile, pushing my leftovers around in my bowl. I wish I had a man who cooked for me. Cooking is something I enjoy, but sometimes I want to be pampered in simple ways – like having someone cook for me and go out of their way to make something I like. "The parent-teacher night was the usual. Lots of helicopter parents. But there was this one dad…" I smile as I remember Roman. The fact is, I haven't been able to stop thinking about him.

"Oooh, a single dad! Was he hot? Tell me he was hot. You need a hot man in your life!" Renee speaks quickly and looks at me, her eyes suddenly bright and filled with excitement.

"Down, girl," I joke. "He was attractive," I say carefully, trying to downplay how magnetically drawn I was to him. Despite being grumptastic, something about Tessa's dad had me clenching my thighs together and trying to remember if my vibrator was fully charged. "But he was a total jerk. His daughter is the most talented writer I've ever had, but he thinks writing is a path to poverty."

Renee puts down her sandwich. "Did you tell him about your books and what you've done?"

"I mentioned it but didn't go into detail. The event last night was about the kids, not about us teachers. Not to mention his mind was already made up, and you know there's no talking to someone like that. Besides, you know if I was a man, he wouldn't have pushed back so hard."

"Sadly, you're probably right," Renee sighs, shaking her head. "You'd think we'd be past that nonsense, but it never ends."

"Yeah. In any case, I invited both of them to the Writing Open House tomorrow night, so hopefully, he'll be open-minded enough to come. If he sees the possibilities and that there's good money in writing, it might be possible to change his mind a little. I mean, look at you. How many long-form investigative pieces have you published nationally now?"

"More than a dozen," she says, blushing. "I haven't told anyone but Coop yet, but I have a book deal!"

"Oh my God, that's amazing! I'm so pleased for you!"

"Thanks," Renee says, beaming. "But back to your student and this hunky dad. For the sake of your student, I sure hope so, Marsha. It's so hard to watch adults who try to stifle what their children are good at."

I nod in agreement. "That's honestly the hardest part of this job. I love teaching, but man, do I want to yell at some of the parents."

"You're doing admirable work, Marsha. Don't you ever forget that. I know how much technical writing jobs pay, and your book royalties are probably nothing to sneeze at. You know this already, but I respect the hell out of you for pursuing your teaching degree and working to encourage kids to write."

I can't help the tears of love and happiness leaking from my eyes this time. Renee knows better than any friend of mine who isn't a writer how hard it can be to pursue a job everyone expects you'll fail at or that will leave you in perpetual poverty.

"Thank you, Renee. I love you, too," I say, wiping my eyes and smiling at her. "That's exactly why I'm doing this. I'm convinced that if we teach children how to express themselves better, people can lead happier lives. Too much bottling things up is only a bomb waiting to explode."

"You don't have to sell me on it." Renee smiles.

"I know. It's just hard not to get worked up about it." I take a moment to center myself. "And thank you for agreeing to come to the Writing Open House. I know there are students who will be thrilled to talk to you."

"Of course. Journalism doesn't pay much, but we still need reporters."

"Don't downplay your achievements," I chide Renee. "Don't you have your second book coming out soon? I've lost count of all those investigative pieces you've been doing. You're living your dream."

"You're right." She beams. "I sent the book to my editor last week! Coop is thrilled because he says I'm finally out of my writing cave for more than meals and sleep."

"I hope one day I find a man who loves me as much as Coop loves you," I say, jealous that she found such a loving man.

"You will," Renee says. "Don't doubt that you're an amazing, intelligent, and stunningly gorgeous woman. If that dad got you so hot and bothered, why not ask him out? What's the worst that could happen?"

"As if," I scoff, but I laugh. "You know I have a rule about not dating single dads. There's inevitably too much drama with the mother of their child, and I'm not sure I have the energy for that. And who says I want to date him?"

"Hm, let's see." Renee grins. "He clearly made an impression on you and sounds like the kind of protective, grumpy man that makes you weak in the knees."

I look away and shake my head. "You know me too well. But, as mentioned, I have no intention of dating a single dad, no matter how much I wanted to jump him."

Renee looks at me for a long moment. "If you felt that strongly about him, maybe you should give it a chance. You've been single a long time, and you're too precious not to have someone to share your life with."

My eyes mist over with love for my friend. We met at a networking event for writers a few years ago and have been fast friends ever since.

"We'll see."

* * *

RENEE'S WORDS play in my head when I'm at home drinking a glass of wine. The strong connection I felt with Roman, even though we only just met, feels…different. It's been so long since I felt that kind of connection with anyone that it's hard not to think that it could mean something.

Then I realize that maybe Renee is right. Maybe it is time for me to take a chance and be open to the possibilities with Roman. I'm sure there will be other times that our paths cross if Tessa remains my student.

The night of the parent-teacher conference, I spotted him across the auditorium and felt my heart skip a beat. I had no idea he was Tessa's dad when I saw him. I remember feeling like all the air in my lungs had disappeared as I watched him. In a crowd of other mothers and fathers, Roman stood out like he was the only person in the auditorium. With his broad shoulders and thick hair, he looked like a bad boy who could make my body melt with just a few kisses. Standing there with his burly dad bod and his wild beard, he looked like a legend come to life.

Roman had this air of authority and no-nonsense, like a man who does an honest day's work and lives with integrity, and it felt like suddenly looking at someone I desperately wanted to have in my life. When I realized who he was and we were speaking, his dark eyes were intense. It seemed as if he was looking for the person I am aside from being his daughter's teacher.

After years of dating men who eventually found reasons to break up with me with flimsy excuses, I stopped feeling like I could trust a man if I were interested in him. Yet with Roman, I instinctively sensed that he was an honorable man I could trust, even though we disagreed about his daughter and writing as a possible career.

Even as we butted heads, I understood he respected me and wasn't arguing to prove he knew my job better than I did.

There was also something about how he looked at me, like he was thinking about saying more but holding back. What might he have said if we had been somewhere more private?

A little tipsy and lightheaded from my wine, my imagination paints vivid pictures of Roman. I envision the tickle of his thick beard as he plants kisses all over my body.

Heat pools between my legs as I imagine his strong hands removing my clothes and exploring every inch of me.

Once I'm in bed, I let myself indulge in my fantasies, trailing my hand over my body and sliding my fingers through the hot slickness at my core. My body trembles as I stroke my swollen bud. My fingers move faster as I imagine Roman making love to me and leaving me breathless. My orgasm suddenly crests, making me moan loudly as I fall back on my pillows.

I catch my breath and snuggle under my covers. Roman is completely unlike any man I've ever met, and the ache of yearning I feel for him makes me want to break my rule about dating single dads.

I mentally shake my head, reminding myself that just because I'm powerfully attracted to the man doesn't mean I should throw caution to the wind.

Yet I'm still left with a certainty that maybe it's time for me to break my rule.

CHAPTER 4

ROMAN

I pull at the neck of my button-down shirt as we walk up to the school's steps. I can't believe I'm at Tessa's school twice in one goddamned week. Every fiber of my being wants to turn around and take Tessa home, but it's obvious how excited she is to come to this. Though I'd be lying if I said I wasn't looking forward to seeing Tessa's teacher again.

Before we walk through the doors to the school, she puts her hand on my arm and stops me.

"What is it, Tessa?"

Her eyes glisten as she looks up at me. "Thanks, Dad. I know you don't want to be here and think I shouldn't, but it means a lot that you agreed to this."

"Well…I…"

"You don't have to say anything, Dad." Tessa smiles and puts her arm through mine.

I open and close my mouth a few times to say something, but this is one of those moments you never understand until you have a kid. No matter how rough it feels to have a teenage daughter who wants to do everything you say she shouldn't, there are moments when I see her heart, and it shakes me to my core. She's a good kid, even if she does have crazy ideas about being a writer.

As we enter the auditorium, she greets a friend with a high-pitched squeal, and I nod as she looks to me for permission to go with her friend to visit all the information booths.

I glance around the auditorium, trying to convince myself I'm not looking for Miss Andrews. She's been stuck in my mind since we met. It's not often a woman has stood up to me, but I haven't been able to stop thinking about her. She may be filling Tessa's head with unrealistic expectations, but it's obvious she's smart.

"You look a bit lost over here." My body stiffens as I feel a hand on my arm, and I turn to see Tessa's English teacher.

"Miss Andrews," I say, my heart suddenly pounding.

"Please," she smiles, "call me Marsha."

Fuck. She's every bit as gorgeous and alluring as I remember. I suck in my stomach, regretting all those beers at the Roadhouse Bar with the guys after work and on the weekends. I resist the urge to tug at my shirt to hide my belly. Marsha is the first woman in a long time I've felt a burning need to impress.

"It's a pleasure to see you again," I say, surprising myself at the formality. "This is quite the event. When you said Writing Open House…this isn't what I expected."

Marsha's pink lips curve into a smile, and she chuckles. "Did you think it would be hippies reciting incomprehensible poetry?"

I look at her, shocked. It's like she understands my fears for Tessa if she pursues writing.

"Are you making fun of me?" I ask, pretty sure she's joking, but I'm so out of my element here that I'm second-guessing everything.

"Only a little." She chuckles. "Let me show you around. I was hoping you would come with Tessa because I also wanted you to see the opportunities."

"Lead the way."

* * *

BY THE TIME Marsha finishes showing me around, my head is pounding. She knows all the professional writers talking to the students and is obviously well-regarded. It's also become apparent that she's downplayed her experience and achievements.

"Is it true that you've written books?" I ask, grateful for a moment of quiet to process everything.

"Indeed it is," she smiles, her eyes filling with pride. "It's mostly under pen names. I love writing, and I've written many different types of things. The pen names are for a bit of privacy."

"What's this technical writing that woman was talking about?" Of all the writers we met, this type of writing seemed the most practical.

"Well, it's exciting. I've done some of that, too."

"How is it you've done all these things? You're young."

Marsha smiles and glances away, waving at a student. "I'm passionate about writing and had a lot of support." When her eyes meet mine again, there's a challenge in them. "I was encouraged to explore writing, and my parents helped me discover the possibilities. The agreement was that I could study creative writing if I double majored in technical writing. My parents were like you," she pauses, making sure I'm paying attention. "They knew how much I loved writing, so they made sure I learned what they called practical writing."

"I have to admit," I say, rubbing my hand roughly over my face and through my beard, "this isn't what I expected. I've heard of some of these types of writing, but I didn't realize there were options like," I gesture at all the booths, "this."

"It's true. You'll also be happy to hear that technical writing, for instance, pays quite well. She can make a six-figure income with a little experience and the right niche. She can do the same thing if she's serious about writing fiction." She pauses, clearly knowing she's dropped an enticing little information nugget at my feet.

I stare at Marsha, my mind working on wrapping itself around this information. "The fuck?" I can't help muttering. Tessa would be making more than I ever have.

Marsha laughs, and when she raises her hand in a wave, I see she's motioning to Tessa. Tessa looks amped up and more excited than I've seen her in a long time. Maybe I do need to loosen up and let her pursue this.

Before she makes it to where Marsha and I are standing, a boy stops her. The blood drains from my face when I see her light up in an entirely different way. Tessa plays with her hair, and it's obvious she's flirting with the boy.

Without realizing it, a growl escapes my mouth, but when I move to take a step to break up Tessa and this boy, Marsha puts her hand firmly on my arm and stops me.

"Leave her be."

"We have an agreement. No dating until she's eighteen. She knows the rules," I say, my voice tight. "She's always been a good kid. I don't know why she's become so headstrong lately."

Marsha shakes her head but smiles warmly. "She's a teenager, Roman. That's what teens *do*. You can't lock her away in a box. I'm not trying to tell you how to parent, but kids need encouragement. Constantly holding them back or saying no to them? Believe me, I've been teaching long enough to know that it rarely works out well. She'll just rebel even more once she gets to college."

I take a deep breath and exhale slowly. "Yeah, that's what one of the guys at work said, that I should give her space and be there to catch her if or when things don't go well."

"You should listen to your friend because that's exactly what she needs. Not everything she wants to do is going to make you happy, but your job is to support her. If she never has a chance to explore her passions and make mistakes, she runs the risk of becoming resentful, which could put a wedge between you two. I see how you are with her, and I've heard how she talks about you – I don't think either of you wants something to jeopardize your relationship."

When Marsha finishes, I turn to face her. She says all this in a matter-of-fact way, but she's not mocking me.

"Do you have kids?"

She laughs. "I have about one hundred of them every day. But no, I don't have kids of my own yet. All of my wisdom comes from watching my students and helping them. I've only been teaching for a few years, but I volunteered at different schools for after-school programs before that. I've seen a lot of students Tessa's age."

I look at Marsha, impressed. Every time we talk, I'm unexpectedly drawn to her and left with a feeling of wanting...no, *needing*, to spend more time with her. It's obvious she cares about Tessa and her other students and is deeply invested in their success. As much as it scares me to consider encouraging Tessa to pursue writing, maybe it's time I listened to Mack and Tessa.

"Dad! Dad!" Tessa bounds over to me.

"What is it, pumpkin?"

"Can I go to the dance on Friday? Please?" She draws out the word please into more syllables than I can count.

"Tessa..." I start, but Marsha catches my eye and gives me a firm stare. "You know, I'll allow it."

"Really?" Tessa's eyes go wide in disbelief. "Are you serious?"

"I am. But," I add before she runs away. "I need to know who you'll be with. I saw you with that boy over there."

"That's Jason. He's in my algebra class."

"I know him. He's a good kid," Marsha says.

I'm both reassured and frustrated that she's interjecting like this and clearly taking Tessa's side. "Okay. Now, you need to be home by eleven. Do I make myself clear?"

"Yes, Dad. I promise I won't be late. Thank you so much!"

I push down the emotion I feel from Tessa jumping in my arms and giving me a bear hug. I love this girl so much that my heart hurts. I've only ever wanted what's best for her and for her to have a better start in life than I did, but maybe it's time to let her spread her wings a little.

"I'm proud of you."

Marsha's voice breaks me from my thoughts of wondering what the hell I just agreed to with Tessa. Maybe Tessa does need more freedom, but knowing that doesn't make it easier to give it to her.

"Thanks." I look at Marsha, and it dawns on me that if I'm letting Tessa break the rules, then I sure as damn well can do the same.

Marsha is magnetic and reminds me how much I miss the company of an intelligent, sexy woman. Not to mention I want to see her with her hair down and away from a bunch of unruly teenagers.

"Marsha, would you like to have dinner with me on Friday?"

CHAPTER 5

MARSHA

*E*arth to Marsha. Earth to Marsha!" I nearly stumble on a crack in the sidewalk when I hear my friend calling my name.

We're taking a walk through the neighborhood on our lunch break because it's one of the first warm days of spring this year.

I jolt at the sound of Helen's laughing voice. "Sorry. Bit distracted. What were you saying?"

I push my tuna sandwich aside, realizing that all the butterflies in my stomach make me not want to touch food.

"Oh, it's nothing important," Helen says, lifting her face to the sun when we pause at a corner. "What's going on with you? You look lost in the clouds."

"Okay, if I tell you, you have to promise not to make a big deal about it." I'm already pre-regretting that I'm going to tell her about my date. Helen teaches math here at Jefferson High and is my closest work friend. "And I mean really swear."

Helen arches an eyebrow and smiles, holding up three fingers like a Girl Scout. "I do solemnly swear not to tease you...much..."

"Fine," I say, rolling my eyes. "Remember how you're always encouraging me to go out with one of the single dads?"

Helen pauses and puts her hand on my arm to stop me from walking. She stares at me with a knowing smile spreading on her face. "You finally did! I'm so happy for you! Who is the lucky guy?"

"You know how I've talked about my student Tessa, the one who's so talented?"

"Isn't her father a grumpy SOB? I've heard about him before."

"He is. He brought Tessa to the Writing Open House, and we talked. He came around a little. I know, I know." I chuckle when I see the surprised look in Helen's eyes. "It was clear how much he loves and is protective over his daughter. But he listened and realized there were more options than being a novelist. He was impressed when he heard how much technical writers can earn."

"Brava, Marsha. Not just for the date but for getting through to him. Parents can be so committed to their beliefs and not open to anything different."

"That's for sure. I also got him to let Tessa go to the dance on Friday, and he asked me out. Said if he was going to let her break the rules by going to the dance, he got to break the rules by asking me out." My heart races thinking about spending the evening with Roman. I've gone through my closet so many times, trying to find the perfect dress to wear.

Helen looks at me for a long moment and nods. "Now are you going out with him to evangelize about the possibilities of writing or the possibilities of some," she winks at me and lowers her voice, "extracurricular activities?"

"Possibly," I say, feeling my cheeks warm.

"*Possibly*, the woman says," Helen jokes, rolling her eyes. "You know, I may be older than you and very happily married, but I still remember what it was like to be young and drawn to someone. Possibly, my you-know-what."

It's hard not to laugh at Helen's censored language. A lot of teachers I've met swear behind closed doors or develop a sanitized set of euphemisms. Helen is the latter.

"Okay, fine. Yes, I'm attracted to him." I exhale. "I don't even understand it."

"Marsha," my friend says gently, "just because you have rules doesn't mean your heart won't break them."

I nod, unable to argue with that. "I know, but it's more than me not wanting to date a single dad. When we met, it was…" I bite my lip at the memory. "It was like everything fired up in my body before we'd even spoken. All that mattered was being close to him. I wanted to touch and smell him, and frankly," I pause, making sure none of the other teachers are eavesdropping, "I felt an overpowering need to do a lot more than that," I say, giving her a knowing look. "He tripped every desire I've ever felt, and some that are new to me."

"That's exactly how it started with Victor and me. The first time we saw each other, we couldn't get enough of each other. He found so many little ways to see me and touch me – pushing back my hair when it was windy, letting his fingers brush against mine, sitting closer than strictly necessary. It felt like the world was gray when we weren't together. Then when we were together, it was technicolor and intoxicating."

What Helen is describing is the very definition of what I've always wanted with a man. After years of not meeting a man like that, I'd consoled myself that maybe my students would have to be the children I'd never have for myself.

"What you've described is how I'm feeling," I admit.

Even thinking about Roman has my heart beating fast and my hormones surging. I don't tell Helen that it's not just that I want to be naked with Roman—I'm drawn to him in a magnetic way that has me wanting more than just hot sex, but to create a life together. I can't even explain how this happened, but one look at him turned on something in me that I couldn't ignore. I barely know the man, but I want the world with him.

"I see you looking all dreamy, Marsha," Helen teases. "If he feels like you do, and in my experience, you only feel like this when the other person feels the same way, you've found someone special. I predict you have a future with this man."

* * *

It's impossible to ignore the butterflies in my stomach as I finish getting ready. I look in the mirror and wonder if this dress is too much, but as I run my hands over the fabric, I decide it's perfect. It's definitely a Date Night Dress, but I can't ignore the self-doubt creeping up inside me. Is Roman really as different as I think he is? I want him to be different from all the other single dads I've met, but my heart wavers. *Am I hoping for too much?*

I give my lashes a final swipe of mascara and blot my lipstick. No matter what my rule is, I can't deny how much I'm attracted to Roman. He has a quiet authority about him, and I love how devoted he is to Tessa and how protective he is of her. I've always wished for someone to be that devoted to me. Even if he's hesitant about Tessa being a writer, it's clear how much he loves her and wants the best for her.

I take a deep breath and shake off my doubts. I have to trust my instincts and give Roman a chance. If I let my insecurities and rules get in the way, I'll ruin everything before it even has a chance to start.

I'm ready to take a chance on him, even if it means breaking my own rule.

CHAPTER 6

ROMAN

*I*f you need anything or any boy messes with you, you call me. Okay, Tessa?"

I look at my daughter and wonder what lunacy it is that I agreed to let her go to the dance tonight. She's pretty in her dress and practically bounces off the walls with excitement at going to her first dance.

"Yes, Dad," she says, but her fake pout can't hide her excitement.

"Your phone is fully charged, right?" I ask, willing myself not to think of all the things that could go wrong. I remember what it was like to be a horny teen boy. Anyone foolish enough to try anything with her will get a quick and devastating lesson on how my daughter should be treated.

"Yes, Dad," Tessa repeats, holding up her phone and showing me. "It'll all be fine. I promise! I'll be with Leslie and Adrianna all night."

"And no boys." I glare at her. I know I'm overprotective, but I don't know any other way to be with my daughter. If it was possible to protect her from all the evils of the world, I'd pay any price to do that. As it is, the best I can do is work to ensure she has a good head on her shoulders and delay as many potential problems as possible.

Tessa meets my stare but nods. She's a good kid, but I also remember how good intentions were easy to ignore when you're in a dark auditorium and dancing with someone who unlocks attractions that overwhelm you with their intensity.

"Look. I know I'm overprotective," I tell Tessa. "I don't want anything bad to happen to you."

She jumps at the sound of her phone buzzing. "Adrianna's here. Thanks for letting me go tonight!"

"You're welcome. I'll pick you up at eleven. Call if anything happens, and I'll be there immediately."

Tessa walks over to me and surprises me with a hug. "I know, Dad. I love you."

"I love you, too," I say, hugging her tightly for a moment, then kissing the top of her head.

* * *

Fuck. Marsha is a bombshell. When she walked into Bella Italia and I saw she was wearing another dress that hugged her curves the way I ache to, my cock instantly tightened. Everything about Marsha makes me want more, and I knew I had to break my rule about being with a woman.

"Do you two know what you'd like to order?" A server silently appears next to our table.

Marsha looks up in surprise. "What do you recommend? Everything looks so good." She folds her menu, an openness in her eyes that reminds me it's been a long time since I've done anything that wasn't planned.

"The chicken piccata is popular, though if you ask me, I love the lasagna. We make the noodles here, but even the staff don't know exactly what goes into the tomato sauce to make it taste like it does."

"That settles it." Marsha chuckles, reaching up to push her wavy brown hair back. "I'll have the lasagna."

"And you, sir?" the server turns to me.

"I'll try the lasagna, too."

"Good choice. Would you like some wine with that?"

Usually, I'm a beer drinker, but when I see Marsha smile like that's her preference, I nod. "I don't know a lot about wine, so whatever you recommend."

"A chianti?" the server offers.

"That would be perfect," Marsha says, smiling as the server nods and leaves our table.

"I'm really a pizza and beer kind of guy," I admit, suddenly uncertain. "I'm a creature of habit, I guess you could say."

"Is that something you picked up in the military?" Marsha puts her arms on the table and leans toward me, and the light of the flickering candles softly illuminates her face. Her blue eyes sparkle as she looks at me, and I know I'm a goner.

"It is. There's something comforting about knowing what you're supposed to do and how you're supposed to do it. I like predictable routines." Other people tease me about how I rely on routine and rules, but admitting this to Marsha feels comfortable, like she's not going to criticize me for it.

Marsha's warm laugh puts me at ease. "Somehow, that's not surprising. I bet it makes Tessa wanting to be a writer much more challenging."

I sigh and nod. "I hadn't thought of it that way, but you're right. I don't understand creativity. There are too many variables for that kind of career."

"I know it can seem scary, but believe me when I say Tessa is talented. I'm not lying about that. However," she says, holding up her hand when she realizes I'm about to interrupt, "your concerns are valid. Being a fiction writer is a hard job, and if she wanted to self-publish, there's a lot more work than just writing. That's why I wanted you both to come to the open house."

"That was eye-opening," I say, remembering the different kinds of writing and how much the salary was for some of them.

"As I hoped it would be. Writing doesn't have to be a one-track career. I'd recommend that Tessa study different kinds of writing and see which one she likes best. That way, she can use her skill for a career that isn't fiction but still lets her do what she's passionate about. There's nothing to stop her from also publishing her stories or writing a novel."

I hesitate for a moment. I've always wanted Tessa to pursue a traditional degree and career, but I'm starting to accept that writing might be her true passion. "I know she's talented, but I worry about whether she'll be successful."

Marsha puts a hand on my arm, and her touch sends shivers down my spine. "So many different kinds of writing jobs pay very well. Tessa is talented. She'll make a great career out of writing."

I look at Marsha, her words sinking in. Maybe it's time for me to start supporting my daughter's dreams, even if they're not what I had in mind for her. She's my little girl, and I love her more than anything, but I realize I need to practice loving her choices even when they differ from what I would choose for her. There's no doubt that she's her own person and has a mind of her own.

"I'm getting the message," I say, smiling warmly at Marsha. I love how passionate she is about supporting Tessa. "Thank you for believing in my daughter."

"It's truly my pleasure," she says, sipping her wine. "Encouraging a student to fulfill their potential, and helping them achieve their dreams, is one of my greatest pleasures."

"What else do you find pleasurable?" I ask, smiling at her.

She pauses for a moment, and color floods her cheeks. I love that I can take her by surprise like this. She's a strong woman, but the glimpses I get of her when I catch her off guard only intensify my desire for her. I want to see her vulnerability and learn what makes her tick. The idea of another man seeing her like this is not something I'm going to let happen willingly. Marsha is going to be mine; rules be damned.

"This," she says, her voice soft. "Tonight. You. This makes me happy."

The openness and vulnerability in her eyes leave me breathless. Reaching across the table, I cover her soft hand with mine. Confusion and fear flood through me when she pulls her hand back.

"Is something wrong? Have I made you uncomfortable?" I have to make this right. Marsha is more than I thought I'd ever find in another woman, and now that I've found her, I'm never letting her go. Whatever it takes to win her over, I'll do.

"Roman," she sighs, her blue eyes glittering in the soft candle-light. "I like you – quite a bit. But I have a rule about dating the single dads of my students."

"You've done this before?" I know her past before meeting me isn't my business, but the idea that I'm not special to her makes me pause.

"No, I have not. That's the thing." She looks me directly in the eyes. "I don't date single dads. Single dads invariably have some kind of drama in their lives because of their exes. I understand Tessa has a mother, but the dynamics of—"

I reach out again and take her hand in mine, holding her firmly so she can't pull away. She needs to hear this. "Marsha, Tessa's mom is out of the picture. Completely. I swear on my life."

The light in Marsha's eyes changes and fills with obvious sadness. "Roman…"

I take a deep breath. Tessa's mom isn't something I like to talk about. "To be honest with you, I didn't know about Tessa until I was discharged from the Army. Melanie never told me she was pregnant. Hell, we'd only dated for a couple of months before I shipped out. We both knew it was a tempo-rary thing. We were young."

"Then what happened?" Marsha is no longer trying to pull her hand away from me, so I know I have to be honest with her.

I rub my free hand over my face and beard. "Melanie," I exhale slowly, counting to five so I don't lose my temper. Marsha hasn't done anything wrong. "When I came back, she dropped Tessa off on my doorstep and told me it was 'my turn' to take care of her. Tessa was in grade school. After getting over the shock of suddenly having a child, I did what a man does – I stepped up and became a dad. Melanie has never come back, and I never want her to. I rarely even think about her."

Marsha looks at me, questions in her eyes. "How does Tessa deal with this? I had the impression her mother wasn't in the picture, but I didn't know what you've just told me."

"Tessa, she's a good kid." I inhale sharply through my teeth. "Most of the time, she's a little trooper, but I know she still has emotions about her mom. Tessa has never forgiven her, and at this point, I'm not sure she ever will. If you ask her, she says she doesn't want to see her."

"That's unfortunate," Marsha says, her eyes glistening.

"It is," I agree. "Melanie didn't do right by either Tessa or me, and as far as I'm concerned, she doesn't exist in our family. Having a family means making sacrifices and supporting one another. You never, ever leave someone behind. Abandoning Tessa is something I can and will never forgive. Believe me when I say Melanie isn't a part of our lives at all and never will be."

We sit for a long moment, and I let Marsha have space to process all of this. I know it sounds harsh, but Melanie lost her right to be Tessa's mom the day she handed Tessa over and disappeared. It took me long enough to deal with my own emotions about her not telling me I was a father.

When Marsha smiles at me, every atom of my body explodes with joy. "Okay. I'm willing to make an exception to my rule. However," she holds up a finger, "I have it on good authority that you have rules about dating. Tessa has told me about how you say she can't date until college."

"She can date when she's thirty," I say gruffly. I'm not sure I'll ever be okay with the idea of a boy touching my daughter.

"She's also told me that the deal is that you agreed not to date, too. How would this work?"

"We're both going to break our rules. If there's one thing I've learned since we met, it's that you are a captivating woman. You're smart, care deeply about Tessa, and are willing to fight for her. And, pardon my language, you're sexy as fuck. If you think I could ever let you walk away from me and out of my life, you are sorely mistaken."

Marsha's face lights up with a sultry smile, and she moves her hand so that she's stroking her fingers over my wrist. Desire builds in me, and there's no way we're ending this date without taking this further. Everything in my body is urging me to claim her, to make her and her sweet curves mine and mine alone.

"I feel the same way about you."

"Good." I exhale with relief. "Because I don't want this to end."

CHAPTER 7

MARSHA

*S*tanding outside the restaurant, I wrap my arms around myself to ward off the chill that has returned to the air. Before I realize what's happening, Roman shrugs out of his coat and wraps it around my shoulders, stepping in front of me to hold his jacket closed.

"Is that better?" he asks, his eyes dropping to my mouth.

In a rush, I'm aware of my breath increasing, my heart skipping along a little faster. Placing my hands over his, I nod. "Thank you. That's much better."

"Good," Roman says, his voice heavy. He's still standing in front of me, and the slight distance between us is driving me nuts.

"I've had a great time with you tonight, Roman. Thank you for asking me out."

"It's absolutely my pleasure, Marsha. You're a beautiful woman."

Roman pushes my hair away from my face, letting his fingers run through my hair so his hand is lightly holding my head. "Me too," he replies in a husky voice, sending shivers down my spine. "I've been wanting to do this all night."

Roman leans in, his lips meeting mine and sending blazing currents of lust through every atom of my being. I moan into his mouth, opening wider to let him kiss me more deeply. Our tongues entwine as our kiss grows in urgency, our bodies pressing together.

We part, gasping for air as we stare into each other's eyes.

Roman looks at me with such intensity that it takes my breath away, and my heart and soul need him more than ever.

"I want you," he whispers, his voice rough with desire.

I smile coyly in response to his words as I run my fingers along his chest. "I want you too," I murmur, running my hands through his hair and stroking his face.

We quickly make our way to his car, and Roman drives through Jefferson. Every time I glance at him, my heart beats faster with anticipation, especially when I see him grinning back at me. I was so hesitant to come on this date, but he's been a wonderful gentleman, and going home with him feels natural and like maybe, just maybe, this could be the start of something magical for us.

As he drives me to his apartment, I see him shifting his gaze between me and the road. His grasp on my hand is firm, and when he touches me, anticipation for what comes next is all I can think about.

At his apartment, he unlocks the door and steps aside for me to enter. I shrug off his coat, hang it on a coat rack, and turn to face him. I reach up and undo the clip holding my hair up, watching with satisfaction as his eyes flare when my hair cascades over my shoulders. His eyes roam across my body, his sexual hunger filling the air between us. His hand slides into mine, leading me through his home, and I follow him without hesitation.

As we reach his bedroom, my core burns with need for Roman. More than anything, I need to feel him between my thighs, feel his cock inside me, rocking with me as we reveal ourselves and share our passion for each other.

Looking into his eyes, I press myself against him and take his face in my hands. Our bodies ignite, our lips meeting in an urgent kiss. His fingers deftly undo the buttons of my dress, and his hands move commandingly over my skin. His mouth trails down my neck, and I let out a low moan, savoring every moment.

"Take me to bed," I moan, wrapping my arms around Roman and pressing my body against his. His heart thumps so hard that I feel its urgent beat through his shirt.

"This way," he says without hesitation, taking my hand and leading me down a short hallway.

Once inside, we go to his bed, and I push him down so he's sitting. Quickly, I straddle him, grinding my hot core against him.

"I've wanted you since I first saw you," I murmur as my fingers trail down his stomach.

He gasps as I undo his belt, and I lean in to kiss him again, the heat growing fiery between us. His tongue roughly probes my mouth, making me moan with passionate desire.

"Is this okay?" I ask as I caress his body. I'm not usually so bold and one to take command, but Roman sparks something in me that makes me want to take control.

"More than okay," he moans, pulling me closer for another passionate kiss. "I never want this to end," he whispers, lifting his fingers to caress my face.

I smile, our lips barely a breath away. "Me, neither," I answer before softly pressing my lips against his.

Roman's hands move to my waist, and before I can catch my breath, he pulls my dress over my head. The air around us fills with electric desire as I watch him admire my body and reach out to caress my bare skin. Roman's hazel eyes meet mine, and I'm overwhelmed by the passion I see.

"Come here," he commands, his voice a husky growl.

I slip out of my bra as I walk toward him, relishing the look in his eyes as he stares at my breasts.

"Goddamn, you're a beautiful woman," he says, reaching for me and pulling me closer.

"Then take off…"

An alarm goes off, and we both startle.

"Is that your phone?" I ask, my mind struggling to see through the haze of lust.

"Dammit!" he says, picking up his phone and turning the alarm off. "I have to go pick up Tessa. The dance is almost over. However," Roman says, gently pulling me to him and holding my breasts up so he can suck at my nipples for a hot moment, "this is not finished. We may not finish this tonight, but we will most definitely continue this another time."

CHAPTER 8

ROMAN

*a*s I wipe thick layers of car oil from my hands on a greasy towel, I notice Mack talking to a tall guy I've never seen before.

"Roman, come over here a minute," Mack asks gruffly.

As I approach, the fluorescent lights overhead casts shadows, and heavy tools clank in the background. Mack and this guy stand beside an old Ford pickup truck with a cracked bumper.

Mack nods at the stranger. "This here is Wes. He's gonna join us starting next week. He just got back from the war."

I offer him a handshake, and he gives me a firm grip. His face is tanned and creased.

"Hey, man. Glad to have you here," I say, meaning it. "We sure can use the extra hands around this place."

"What all do you work on here?" Wes asks, looking around at all the cars.

"We do all kinds of work here; oil changes, brake jobs, engine swaps, you name it. We even do customizations and restore old cars."

Mack crosses his arms over his barrel chest and smiles with pride. "This ain't the fanciest place around, but we get the job done right every time. There's not much we can't fix. People from all over the Heartland region come to us because they know they can rely on us and we won't gouge them on price. Isn't that right, Roman?"

"That's right, boss," I reply, turning back to Wes. "You work on vehicles in the Army?"

Wes nods. "I specialized in heavy-duty diesel engines. I worked on tanks, Humvees—you name it."

"He's got a knack for computers too, so he'll be able to work on some of those newer cars if they come through," Mack says, then turns back to Wes. "You've got plenty of experience, so you'll be a great addition to our team."

"Welcome to the family, Wes. You need anything, you let me know," I tell Wes. I recognize the look of him from other men I met in the service. He knows how to do his job, and doing it to the best of his ability is what drives him.

"Okay, Roman, can you show Wes around?"

"Sure thing, boss."

After giving Wes a garage tour, I walk him out to the street.

"Thanks, Roman," Wes says, squinting at the Rebel Autos sign on the front of the building. "I think I'm going to like it here."

"We're glad to have you. We've been short-handed for a while now. What brings you to Jefferson?"

Wes rubs his hand roughly over his face and shakes his head. "I was planning to head to San Diego when I got out. Good weather, nice beaches for watching the ladies."

I chuckle. "Yeah, babes in bikinis. What made you say no to that?"

"Buddy of mine. Before he went on a mission we all knew was dangerous, he made me promise to look after his little girl if it all went to shit." Wes pauses for a long moment, the cloud falling over his face telling me what happened. "Slade nailed the mission, then those fuckers nailed him with a fucking IED on a road in the middle of nowhere when he was coming back to base. There wasn't enough of him left to send home."

I shake my head, then put my hand on his shoulder. Everyone who's been out in the desert has stories like this, and I also lost buddies of mine to IEDs. "I'm real sorry to hear that, man. How old's this girl you came here for? Her mom in the picture?"

"I haven't met her yet. She won't answer my calls, and it's a crapshoot if she responds to a text. From what Slade told me, she should've had her twenty-first birthday recently. Her mom died from breast cancer a couple of years back." Wes's voice chokes a little, and I let him take his time catching his breath. "Her death is what prompted him to do another tour. His version of dealing with hard shit was to fight, and the Army gave him ample opportunity for that."

"That's a lot to deal with. I've been where you are now. You need to talk or shoot the shit or someone to buy the beers on a Friday night and not say a word about the past, I'm your man."

Wes meets my eyes and nods. His eyes are filled with turmoil and loss.

"Appreciate it, Roman. I'll take you up on that. In the meantime, thanks for the tour. I'll see you next week." Wes gives me a sharp nod, then turns and walks down the street, his hands shoved deep in the pockets of his Army jacket.

I go back inside the garage and focus on fixing the car I'm working on. Serving my country is something I grew up knowing that I'd do, but the things that happen in war can haunt a man. It's been a while since I served, but watching Wes talk about his buddy stirs up a lot of emotions – emotions I have done just fine ignoring.

What are we living for? What if everything went up in flames tomorrow? Would I be happy? As a father, yes. No matter how much Tessa pushes boundaries, she's a good kid, and I'm proud as hell of her. She has a good head on her shoulders.

But Marsha. There's no denying the attraction between us. If something happened tomorrow, I'd regret not breaking my damn rules and asking her to join my life – to join the life Tessa and I share.

I wish dealing with emotions was as straightforward as working on a car. There's no guesswork in working on an older car – the parts aren't a mystery, you just put them together in the right way, and it all works. With emotions, they leave me feeling exposed and vulnerable, which is something the Army trained me not to do.

Yet the memory of having Marsha in my arms and nearly in my bed replays in my head over and over; her hands on my body, her lips pressed against mine, the scent of her hair as I pulled her closer, how she took control, and how I loved it when I started to let myself be vulnerable. I wanted to give myself to her, not just for one night.

What kind of example am I setting for Tessa if I break my own rules?

I wonder what would have happened if we'd finished what we started. Would it be enough to satisfy our desire, or would it only make things worse? The thought of us being together forever is tempting, yet so far-fetched at the same time. We barely know each other, but the attraction between us is staggering.

Friday night, I thought I wanted nothing more than to feel her tight pussy wrapped around my throbbing cock. Good chemistry means good sex.

Then it hits me like a sledgehammer. One night with Marsha isn't enough, and it will never be enough. I want more than just good sex.

I need Marsha in my life forever.

* * *

"We need to talk," I tell my daughter.

Tessa looks at me and has the good sense not to roll her eyes, which has been an unfortunate habit of late.

"What is it, Dad?"

I take a deep breath and try to explain in the most appropriate way possible, "I have strong feelings for your teacher, Miss Andrews. I know this might seem strange to you, but I wanted to talk it out with you before taking any steps."

Tessa takes a few moments to consider my words before she responds. "Are you asking me if I think it's weird?"

I nod. "Yes, sweetheart. Is this something that would bother you? Do you have any objections?"

Tessa thinks for a minute, shifting her weight from one leg to the other. She bites her lip. "No, Dad," she says, shaking her head slightly, "I don't think it's weird at all."

I nod, relieved that she's not going to make a scene over it. It's not like I even need to tell her, but if this goes how I hope it will, I need to know my daughter is on board with this.

Tessa pauses, then continues. "In fact, I think it's kind of sweet that you have these feelings for someone. But... Are you sure this is what you want? I mean, does Miss Andrews feel the same way about you?"

I take a moment to consider her question before I answer. It's not like I'm going to tell my daughter that Marsha was here on Friday night, and we nearly made love. "I'm not sure how she feels, but I know how I feel, and...yes, this is exactly what I want. I intend to find out."

Tessa thinks for a moment, then narrows her eyes at me. "So if you get to date someone, does that mean I can, too?"

There's a look of excitement in Tessa's eyes, and I feel conflicted. If I break one of my rules, she's probably expecting that she can do the same.

"Look. I know we have rules..."

"No, Dad. You have rules. I have to live with them."

I take a deep breath before asking, "Tessa, is there a boy you're interested in?"

"Not particularly," she says thoughtfully.

"Okay, so if it's not a boy, what do you want?" I ask, already dreading the answer.

Tessa pauses for a moment before answering. "I want to go to the summer writing conference that Miss Andrews mentioned to me."

I push down the automatic refusal on the tip of my tongue. *Be open to the possibilities and support Tessa*, I hear Mack and Marsha reminding me. I know Tessa is passionate about writing, and this could be something special for her.

"Okay," I finally say, taking one last deep breath. "I'll think about it. Email me the info for the program, and I'll see what we can do."

Tessa looks at me with such hope that my heart contracts with love.

"Thank you so much, Dad. It's a deal!" Tessa jumps up and hugs me, and it makes me love her even more. "But," she says, stepping away and looking at me with puppy dog eyes. "Can I ask for one more thing?"

"Go on," I say, folding my arms over my chest.

"Carmen is having a sleepover on Saturday night. Can I go? Please? Please?"

"Conditionally, yes. I need to talk to the parents for Carmen, but I think we can do this.

This is part of why I've always wanted rules for Tessa and for me. Once you start deviating from them, everything can spiral until you're lost. Everything with Marsha reminds me that life doesn't fit into nice little rules and that I have to let Tessa be a kid and do everyday things. It doesn't make it easier for me, but I have to trust that I've taught the right lessons to Tessa and that she'll make smart decisions. And if she doesn't, I'll be here to help her put everything back together.

"Okay. Go to your room, and don't make me regret this," I joke. She knows that once I give it, my word is my bond. In my mind, she's allowed to go to the sleepover because I know exactly what I want to do and who I want to see, alone and without distractions. "I have a phone call to make."

* * *

"Marsha, how are you?" I sit on my couch, pressing my hand against my knee to stop it from bouncing. Just hearing her voice again has me feeling like a teenager. I know how to talk to women. I know how to ask a woman out. But with Marsha, the stakes are higher.

"Roman, hello. What can I do for you? Is everything okay with Tessa?"

I nod, then realize she can't see me through the phone. "Tessa's fine. She's just finishing up some homework for tomorrow. I called because," my knee bounces harder, "I wanted to invite you for dinner this Saturday night. I'm cooking."

"Oh," she says, her voice filled with surprise. "I don't usually have dinner with students and their parents."

"Ah, Tessa is going to a sleepover that night. This would just be the two of us." I take a deep breath. "Would you let me cook dinner for you?"

CHAPTER 9

MARSHA

*T*hat was amazing," I say, taking a sip of my beer and looking across the table at Roman. My heart wanted to accept his dinner invitation, but my mind was telling me I was making a mistake, even after our hot first date.

"I'm glad you approve." Roman's voice is teasing as he clears the plates. "Why don't you have a seat on the couch, and I'll be over in a sec."

Smiling, I get up and make my way to the couch. Now that I've had a chance to look at more than his bedroom, I'm impressed with the home he has with Tessa. Everything is clean and tidy, which is certainly influenced by Roman's time in the Army. Pictures of Tessa hang around the living room, along with a large picture of Roman and several other smiling men in Army uniforms. I'm guessing it was taken shortly after he graduated from basic training because the buttons on his uniform jacket are shiny, and everyone in the picture looks jazzed and energetic.

"Is this your... I'm afraid I don't remember the right word. Troop?"

"Squad," Roman calls out. I look at him as he wipes his hands on a dishtowel, and my heart beats faster. "And yes, those are the guys I deployed with. We look like grinning idiots, don't we?"

Roman comes over to me and drapes her arm over my shoulder. I instinctively lean into him. Everything about him feels so right that it takes my breath away.

"You know," I say, pulling away slightly so I can look into his eyes. "I love that you cooked for me tonight. Thank you."

Roman turns to face me, his hazel eyes intense as they meet mine. "You're welcome, Marsha. It's my pleasure."

"A girl could get used to this." My tone is teasing, but there's so much truth to this that my heart aches for it to be true.

"Let's sit." Roman leads me to the couch and sits in the recliner across from where I'm sitting. "About us."

"Yes?" I ask, my stomach tensing. My heart tells me I haven't misread things with Roman, but my logical mind is butting in again and telling me this is all a mistake. "Is this about last week?"

"In part, yes. Marsha," he says, leaning toward me and reaching for my hands. "You're a remarkable woman. I want you in my life."

"Really?"

"I mean," he grins, "I know I'm not some fashion model, and my stomach is a little soft these days, but there's more than physical attraction between us. That's how it feels to me."

I exhale and nod, my heart thumping. "That's how it feels to me, too. I just wasn't sure that I could trust how my heart felt."

Roman smiles and moves so that he's sitting next to me. "How has your heart felt?"

"It feels like rushing headlong into something both terrifying and wonderful. It scares me a little how instantly I was attracted to you and how I'm more attracted to you every time I see you. And not," I smile at him, "just because you have a hot dad bod, but because I'm falling for the person you are, too."

"I like the sound of this," Roman says, gently pushing my hair behind my ear. He lightly traces his fingers down the side of my throat and along my collarbone, making me shiver with desire. "I feel the same way about you too, Marsha. I've had this rule that I wouldn't date anyone until Tessa was in college, but I can't wait that long for you. I need you in my life now, in our life. Tessa likes you, and I know that you'll be an excellent influence on her."

"Even if I encourage her to pursue creative writing?" I tease.

Roman chuckles and nods, "Even if you do that, as long as you encourage her to study technical writing or one of those other professional writing niches we saw at the open house."

"That's a plan I can get behind," I say, turning and looking into Roman's eyes.

"I'm glad you feel that way, Marsha, because believe me when I tell you that I'm sure about you, and I'm sure about us. I want this to be the beginning of something that will last forever."

"I like the sound of that," I tell Roman, reaching out, putting my hand on his strong thigh, and smiling when he flexes it for me. "I had a rule, too, you know. I always said that I wouldn't date a single father, but then I saw you at the parent-teacher conference, even before Tessa introduced us, and you just took my breath away. I knew then how attracted I was to you because I could see the kind of strong, good man you are, even without hearing you say a word. And having you cook for me is just the cherry on top."

"If I can make you smile like that every night for the rest of our lives, then I will cook for you every night for the rest of our lives," he says.

"Oh, Roman," I say, my eyes feeling misty from joy. "You are more than I ever hoped to find in a man."

"Come here, you gorgeous woman," he whispers. "I've been wanting to do this all night."

Roman lowers his mouth to mine, and my core aches with hot arousal as his tongue pushes past my lips and strokes mine passionately. I want Roman more than I thought it was possible to want another person.

Our kiss deepens, and I moan as his tongue teases me, making me yearn to be in bed with him. His hands make their way across my chest, and I shudder in delight.

"Let's continue what we started last week." Roman's voice is thick with desire as he rises and holds my hand for me to stand, too. He kisses my lips lightly, then kisses my ear and my throat, and my knees go weak. "This time," he says, his fingers reaching under my blouse and caressing my skin, "we have all night. No one is going to interrupt us."

Roman leads me into his bedroom, and we race to undress and get into bed. We roll to face each other in bed, and a heady combination of lust and love fill me. I move on top so I'm straddling him and gasp when his hard cock bumps and pushes at my entrance, twitching as my slick core bears down on him.

Without a doubt, I know this is right. I know that being with Roman is right. We begin kissing again, with an intensity that shakes me to the bottom of my soul.

The power with which I want him inside me is a primal urge. Nothing could stop me from making love to Roman tonight. I know now that a life with Roman and Tessa is what I want. I want to build a life with them and become a family.

"I want you so much," I moan. My fingers wrap around his length, and I shiver as he groans with delight. I trace my finger along the tip and feel it pulse beneath my touch as his desire grows even more intense.

"I want you too," he growls into my ear, sending a wave of pleasure through my body.

Roman's strong hands grip my waist, and a shiver of pleasure passes through me. I lower myself onto him, feeling my core clench at his thick length. Roman holds me tightly against his chest, and explosions of pleasure go off as he begins to fill me. Our bodies move together, each stroke of his cock sending shockwaves of pleasure through every cell in my body. *This*. This is what I've wanted and searched for so long to find.

A raw, relentless desire takes over as he moves within me, his thrusts pushing me further and further to the brink of ecstasy. His hot breath tickles my ear as he wraps his arms around me and holds me fiercely as we move together, gasping and groaning as our furious lovemaking reaches a fever pitch. Intensity builds inside me, and I know my orgasm is drawing near.

"I'm coming! Oh my God! I'm coming! Roman!" My breaths come out in shallow gasps as my orgasm opens and crashes through my body. He thrusts into me faster, creating an intense internal drum beat that intensifies my orgasm, and I cry out as my body bucks against his, taking his thick cock deep inside me.

"I can't hold back any longer!" Roman's voice is thick and uneven as he rolls me onto my back and thrusts deeply and wildly inside me.

I moan as his body shakes as he comes. Roman collapses next to me, wrapping one arm over my breasts possessively and threading one of his legs through mine. I hold onto him tightly, unable to let go.

"You are incredible, Marsha." Roman kisses my neck, and I squirm from being tickled by his beard. His fingers find my nipples, and I moan and arch into his touch. His fingers gently pinch and pull at my nipples, and a new flame of desire is lit inside me.

"We're not going to get any sleep tonight. You know that, right?" I look at Roman, my happiness at this moment so much stronger than I thought possible.

"I like the sound of that. I love you, Marsha." Roman moves his body over mine, holding himself up with his strong arms.

"I love you, too, Roman. Now kiss me and make love to me again."

* * *

EPILOGUE

*Y*ou be good now, you hear?" Roman tells Tessa, who grins and nods her head vigorously. She hitches her backpack higher as she looks at the crowd of students.

"I will, Dad, I promise. Thank you so much. I love you!" Tessa wraps her arms around Roman, giving him a huge hug. I can hear his breathing catch as he hugs her back and kisses the top of her head.

"I believe in you Tessa. We're just going to be on the coast, so give us a call if anything happens," Roman says and she nods.

"She'll be fine," I say, threading my arm through his.

Tessa looks at me and my heart swells with love for her, too. I've always heard nightmares about friends who dated men with a teenager and how the teenager made their life a living hell. But Tessa has welcomed me in a way that has surprised me and made my heart expand with love for her.

"Come here, you," I tell Tessa, then give her a big hug. I whisper in her ear, "you're going to love it here. I'm so glad you have this opportunity."

She steps back and pride swells in me. This is exactly the right environment for her and I'm proud that Roman came around to approving this. She needs that kind of support in her life.

We watch as Tessa walks down the hall, joining a group of other teens like herself, but then turns and waves back at us.

"Remind me again how she's going to be okay?" Roman asks as we walk back to the rental car. He's jingling the car keys in a way that reveals how nervous he is.

"She'll do great. I know the director of the program and they're used to looking out for these kids," I say, trying to reassure him.

"It's my first time being apart from her," Roman's voice catches as he pulls out of the parking lot. "It's harder than I thought it would be."

"I understand, sweetie, I do." I put my hand on his thigh as he drives. Even though our relationship is still new, we're always finding a way to be physically connected when we're together. It makes me smile because it's exactly what Helen described about how it was when she met her husband.

"How long until we get to the coast?" I ask, rolling down the window and enjoying the warm summer air.

"GPS says it should be about two hours."

***

"This place is fantastic," I say, the sound of the surf reaching us before we can see the ocean. We turn through a stand of trees, and the ocean is suddenly there, bold and magnificent.

Waves are crashing on the beach and there are people flying kites high in the sky. It looks like the very definition of summer.

"Yeah, it's not bad," Roman says, grabbing our bags from the trunk and bringing them to the door.

"Here we go." I punch in a code on a keypad and the door clicks open, revealing a beautiful, open-style living room with exposed wood beams, with a couch facing a huge fireplace. To our right is the kitchen with granite countertops, stainless steel appliances and a large island.

"Wow," I say, taking it all in. "It's even better than the pictures."

Roman laughs as he drops our bags in the corner, then goes back to the car to grab the groceries we picked up in town.

After he finishes stocking up the kitchen, Roman comes up behind me and wraps me in a big hug as I stand at the front door and look out at the ocean. I lean back into him, his beard tangling with my curly hair. The warmth of his embrace makes me happier than anything else in the world.

Roman is my rock. He is exactly the man he says he is and he loves me with a passion that feels like winning the lottery each and every day of my life. Each day with him and Tessa is a gift.

"What are you cooking tonight?" I can't help but grin as I look at the man I love. He doesn't do it every night, but he does cook for me regularly. I'm not a bad cook -- he just loves to pamper me.

"If memory serves, there's a grill outside. Steak and grilled corn sound good to you?"

"Sounds perfect. How about you get started and I'll unpack our clothes?"

"Deal."

***

"I love how you spoil me."

Roman rubs my shoulders as we sit on the porch of the cabin, sipping our beers as we watch the sunset.

The sun glows on the horizon as it slowly sinks. The waves continue to crash on the beach, the sound louder now that the tide is coming in.

I rest my head against Roman's chest, savoring his embrace. As much as I love Tessa, I'm grateful that we'll have this week to ourselves.

"We should head in," I say, rubbing my arms against the sudden chill of the night air.

As Roman builds a fire in the fireplace, I make us hot chocolate with rum.

"This is delicious," Roman says, putting down his mug and pulling me into his arms. I draw circles on his thigh with my finger, giggling when he flexes his muscles for me. No matter how often he does it, it always makes me happy.

"Thanks." I lean in to kiss him, but he pulls away. "What? No kissing?" I tease, though confused. It's not often we pull away from each other.

Roman clears his throat and moves so that we're facing each other on the couch.

"Marsha, I love you." Roman's hazel eyes twinkle in the fire-light and I reach up to rub my hand over his jaw and beard.

"I love you, too, Roman. I always will."

"I can't imagine my life without you and I never want to. The way you are with Tessa is beautiful to watch. I love how supportive and patient you are with her, and how much she respects and cares for you, too."

Roman takes my hands in his, his hazel eyes never leaving mine.

"I love her, too, Roman. You know that." My voice catches from the intensity of the moment. You don't normally know the moments that will change your life, but I know this is one of them -- and I'm ready for this.

"Marsha, having you come into our lives makes me the happiest man on earth." Roman moves off the couch and gets down on one knee in front of me, his eyes never leaving mine.

"Oh, Roman." My voice is jagged from emotion as he holds my hands in his and looks up into my eyes. The vulnerability in his eyes makes me tremble.

"Marsha, would you do me the honor of spending the rest of our lives together? Every moment with you is precious and I want to make every moment count." Roman's voice catches as he lets go of my hands, then reaches into his pocket and pulls out a red velvet box. "Will you marry me?"

Roman opens the box and the firelight makes the diamond ring sparkle brighter than the stars in the sky. My love for Roman overflows my heart and I nod, tears of joy streaming down my face.

"Yes, Roman. Yes!" My fingers tremble as Roman slides the ring on my finger, then tenderly kisses each fingertip on my left hand. "There aren't words to describe how much I love you, Roman."

I pull him up and our kiss explodes with passion. Each stroke of his tongue sends ripples of desire across my skin.

We quickly undress, and then Roman gently lowers me onto the sheepskin rug in front of the fireplace.

Stroking my face, he looks at me with pure adoration.

"You are the most beautiful woman in the world," he says, moving his body over mine.

"And you are the most handsome, sexiest man I've ever laid eyes on." I reach up and pull his mouth down to mine, gasping at the intensity of our kiss.

Roman's hands caress my body, lingering over my wide hips. "I love your curves, Marsha. Every one of them."

I smile up at Roman and spread my legs for him. His thick cock twitches against my hot core, and I instinctively raise my hips up to him. I need him inside me with a desire that's blinding.

"We have the whole week to ourselves," Roman says, his eyes twinkling with anticipation.

"Let's make it one to remember," I whisper, crying out as he thrusts into me.

Our bodies move in a frantic rhythm, the heat from the fireplace glowing on our skin. I grind against him, pushing my hips up so I can take all of him even deeper.

In a blinding burst of pleasure, my orgasm comes fast and intense, making me see stars.

"Oh my God!" I cry out, wrapping my arms around Roman as he pumps faster and faster, his groans echoing in the cabin as he comes and his body shakes over mine.

"I love you, Marsha."

"I love you, too. Roman. Now and forever."

* * *

THANK **you so much for reading** *Dad Bod Rebel*!

To read the rest of the books in this series, please visit:

https://www.amazon.com/dp/B0BVRQHN7C

If you enjoyed *Dad Bod Rebel*, please leave a review on your favorite retailer, Goodreads, or Bookbub! Your feedback helps other readers find my books and lets me know which books you like best!

Want a free book? Join my newsletter and receive *Sweet Temptation*! Subscribers are the first to hear about new releases, sales, and freebies!

https://dl.bookfunnel.com/bdh6jsgeyo

Want to read Wes and Kira's story? Preorder *A Rebel's Honor* today!

https://www.amazon.com/dp/B0C3F1N98M

This book is part of the **Heartland Heroes** world.

For more Lana Love books, please visit:

https://www.amazon.com/Lana-Love/e/B078KKRB1T/

https://www.loveheartbooks.com

ABOUT LANA LOVE

Lana Love is a USA Today Bestselling Author of steamy stories about relatable women, and the strong men who will move heaven and earth to capture the heart of the curvy woman they can't live without. Curvy since forever, Lana writes the heroines she never read about or saw in movies when she was growing up.

Lana lives in the Pacific Northwest and is passionate about dancing, travel, chocolate, and cocktails, and writing stories that make her heart race and bring her fantasies to life. She loves a man who loves curves and who knows what to do with them!

For books with relatable women, sinfully hot men, and steam that will melt your e-reader, you've found a new favorite author!

https://www.loveheartbooks.com

You can follow me on social media at:

https://www.goodreads.com/author/show/12219675.Lana_Love

https://www.bookbub.com/profile/lana-love

https://www.facebook.com/groups/746330989530967

Ingram Content Group UK Ltd.
Milton Keynes UK
UKHW040917080623
423095UK00001B/7

9 798223 753452